About the Book

GEORGE W. ALLEN was proud of two things. His name and his birthday. He was named for George Washington and he had the same birthday. It made him feel almost related. So related he wanted to know everything he could about George Washington.

George wanted to know the *important* things — he already knew the names of Washington's dogs and what size shoes he wore, but he didn't know what George Washington ate for breakfast. He got his grandmother to promise she'd cook George Washington's breakfast if he found out what it was, and he was going to find out — no matter what.

The whole family and even the town librarian joined George in his search, which included exploring sources from the card catalogue to a trip to Mount Vernon. Told with humor and a keen sense of factual detail, this story brings history to life with a freshness and excitement that will delight every child. Paul Galdone's colorful illustrations are rich in historical accuracy as well as lively imagination.

About the Author

JEAN FRITZ is the distinguished author of books for young people, most of which deal with American history. They include several novels and biographies of Paul Revere, Sam Adams, Patrick Henry, John Hancock, Ben Franklin and George III, as well as Stonewall Jackson, Benedict Arnold and Pocahontas. In 1982 her book *Homesick: My Own Story* won the American Book Award and was a Newbery Honor Book. Ms. Fritz and her husband live in Dobbs Ferry, New York.

About the Artist

PAUL GALDONE has retold and illustrated close to twenty classic tales, as well as illustrating another ten books, two of which were written by his daughter Joanna. He was born in Hungary and came to the United States at the age of fourteen. He studied at the Art Students League in New York City. Mr. Galdone and his wife divide their time between their Vermont farm and a home in Rockland County, New York.

George Washington's Breakfast

by Jean Fritz

Paul Galdone drew the pictures

COWARD-McCANN, INC.   NEW YORK

For
Carol Louise Kelly

Grateful acknowledgment is made to the Mattatuck Historical Association of Waterbury, Connecticut, and to Mr.
Rawson W. Haddon for the title and the idea of this book,
taken from *George Washington's Breakfast*, Occasional Pub-
lications, No. 26.

Text copyright © 1969 by Jean Fritz.
Illustrations copyright © 1969 by Paul Galdone.
Published simultaneously in Canada.
Printed in the United States of America.
Library of Congress Catalog Card Number: 69-11475
ISBN 0-698-30099-8 (hc)
11   13   15   17   19   20   18   16   14   12
First paperback edition, 1984.
ISBN 0-698-20616-9 (pbk)
7   9   10   8

George Washington's
Breakfast

George W. Allen was proud of two things.
His name and his birthday.

George was named for George Washington. And he had
the same birthday. February 22.

It made him feel almost related, he said.

It made him want to know everything there was to know
about George Washington.

Already he knew quite a lot. He knew that Washington was a general and lived in Virginia and was six feet tall and married to Martha and was the first President of the United States.

He knew that Washington rode two horses in the war, Blueskin and Nelson, but Nelson was his favorite because he was so steady in gunfire.

He also knew that Washington once had ten hunting dogs.
Their names were: Tipsey, Pompey, Harry, Maiden, Lady,
Dutchess, Drunkard, Tru-Love, Mopsy, and Pilot.

Then one day at breakfast George Allen thought of something he didn't know. George's mother and father had gone to work, and his grandmother was frying eggs at the kitchen stove.

"Grandma," George said, "what did George Washington eat for breakfast?"

"Search me," his grandmother said. "That was before my time." She put a plate of fried eggs in front of George. "And don't you expect me to help you find out either."

George's grandmother knew what George was like. When George wanted to find out something, he didn't rest until he found out. He didn't let anyone else rest either. He did just what his grandfather used to do — ask questions, collect books, and pester everyone for answers. And George's grandmother wasn't going to fool around now about breakfasts that were over and done with two hundred years ago. Besides, there was the spring housecleaning to do.

George punctured the two fried eggs on his plate. "Well," he said, "if I find out, will you do one thing for me?"

"What's that?"

"Will you cook me George Washington's breakfast?"

George's grandmother looked at the clock on the kitchen wall. "George," she said, "you'll be late for school."

"But will you?" George insisted. "Will you cook me George Washington's breakfast?"

George's grandmother was still looking at the clock. "I'll cook anything," she said, "as long as you hurry."

After school that day George Allen went to the library. Miss Willing, the librarian, smiled when she saw him come in the door. "I wonder what that Allen boy wants to know now," she thought.

George walked up to the desk. "Miss Willing," he said, "do you know what George Washington ate for breakfast?"

Miss Willing could hardly remember what *she'd* had for breakfast that morning, but like George, she liked to find out answers.

Together George and Miss Willing went to the encyclopedia and looked under *W*. "Washington, George." The encyclopedia said Washington was born in 1732, married in 1759, elected President in 1789 and died in 1799. It told all about the years when he took trips and fought battles and did other important things. But it didn't say what he did everyday. It didn't mention his breakfasts.

Miss Willing took George to the card catalogue where every book in the whole library was written down on a separate card with a number or letter that told where you could find it. George liked opening the little drawers of the catalogue and finding the right drawer and flipping through the cards until he found what he wanted. There were seven books about George Washington. Most of them were in the section of the library marked *B* for Biography.

George picked out four books to take home, and Miss Willing promised that she would look at the rest.

HOURS
MONDAY 10-9
TUESDAY 10-9
WEDNESDAY 10-2
THURSDAY 10-9
FRIDAY 10-5
SATURDAY 10-5

NEW CITY
FREE LIBRARY

That night after supper George gave his father a book to read, and he gave his mother a book to read.

"Don't look at me," his grandmother said. "I said I'd cook but I wouldn't look."

So George kept the other two books for himself. All evening George and his mother and father read.

George was very excited when he found out that Washington liked to count things. George liked to count things too. George had counted how many steps there were between his house and the school. And there was Washington back in the 1700's counting steps too! It made George feel more related than ever.

The book said that once Washington figured out that there were 71,000 seeds in a pound of red clover. And 844,800 seeds in a pound of Red River grass.

But there wasn't a word about Washington's breakfasts, and the way George figured it, Washington must have eaten breakfast more than 24,000 times.

Then all at once Mrs. Allen looked up. "Listen to this," she said. "This book says that in Washington's time breakfast in Virginia usually consisted of cold turkey, cold meat, fried hominy, toast, cider, ham, bread and butter, tea, coffee and chocolate."

George Allen felt his mouth beginning to water. He grinned and looked at his grandmother.

"Humph!" his grandmother scoffed. "Notice the book said what was *usual* in Virginia. Everyone knows George Washington was an unusual man. No telling what he ate."

A little later Mr. Allen looked up from his book. "Guess what?" he said. "It says here that people in Washington's day didn't eat a real breakfast. Instead they had lunch at ten o'clock in the morning."

George Allen's grandmother grinned and looked at George.

"Doesn't mean a thing," George said. "That book's talking about Washington's day. Not about George Washington."

The day the Allens finished reading their four books was a Saturday, a nice, sunny spring Saturday. George Allen's grandmother took down the curtains to wash. His mother hung the winter clothes outside.

George went back to the library. Miss Willing suggested that they find out what some of George Washington's friends had to say.

First they read from the diary of John Adams, who was the second President of the United States. John Adams wrote that George Washington ruined his teeth when he was a boy by cracking walnuts in his mouth.

Thomas Jefferson, the third President of the United States, wrote that Washington was the best horseman of his age.

General Lafayette, who helped Washington fight the Revolutionary War, wrote that George Washington wore a size

13 shoe and had the biggest hands he'd ever seen. It was said that he could bend a horseshoe with his bare hands.

No one mentioned if George Washington ever ate or not.

Day after day George and his mother and father and Miss Willing read. George's grandmother started to clean the attic.

Then one day Miss Willing said the reading was over. There were no more books in the library about George Washington. Of course there were bigger libraries, she pointed out. George could go to one of them.

But George had a different idea. "We'll go to Washington's home in Mount Vernon, Virginia," he said, "where George Washington's breakfasts were actually cooked."

The next weekend George and Mr. and Mrs. Allen got in the car. They asked George's grandmother to come, but she said, no, she'd cook, but she wouldn't look. Besides, she was glad to get rid of them, she said. She'd have the attic to herself. No one could poke around trying to rescue things that should be thrown out.

On the way to Mount Vernon, George and his mother and father stopped at Washington, D.C. George wanted to go to the Smithsonian Institution, a museum that had all kinds of historical exhibits — log cabins, covered wagons, and glass cases full of old guns and old coins and old knives and old watches.

"You won't find George Washington's breakfast here," Mr. Allen said. "He ate his breakfasts. He didn't put them in a glass case."

George said that in such a big museum a person couldn't tell what he'd find.

He didn't expect to see George Washington himself, and he certainly didn't expect to see him dressed in a curtain. George's father said that Washington was wearing a Roman toga. Not that he had ever worn a Roman toga, but the sculptor thought he'd look nice in it. George wondered if Washington was embarrassed by the toga, but he decided he wasn't. Washington looked calm and rather satisfied, George thought. As a matter of fact, Washington looked as if he'd just eaten a nice breakfast. But there was no way to tell what the breakfast was. There was nothing in the museum that told about Washington's breakfast.

Still, George did see the uniform that Washington wore on December 23, 1783, when he resigned from the Army. It was a black and tan uniform, and it had white ruffles and brass buttons. Every place George looked there were brass buttons — down the front of the jacket, on the vest, at the back of the neck, on the sleeves and pockets, on the tails of the coat and at the knees. George walked all around the uniform and counted the buttons. There were 64 brass buttons.

Then George walked back to the statue. "I bet you and I," he said, "are the only ones in the world who ever counted up all those buttons."

At Mount Vernon George and his mother and father went right to the kitchen. They walked on the same path that Washington had walked on, and every time George put his feet down, he thought of Washington's size 13's in the same spot.

The kitchen was in a separate building at the side of the house. It was a large room with a big brick fireplace at one end and brass pots and iron pots and griddles and pans and ladles hanging on the walls. George held his breath. It was at that very fireplace, he told himself, that Washington's breakfasts had been cooked. The food may actually have been in some of those very pots and pans. Suddenly George felt so related to Washington that goose pimples broke out on his arm.

He turned to a guard in uniform standing at the door. "Can you tell me," George said, "what George Washington ate for breakfast?"

The guard spoke as if he were reciting a lesson. "Breakfast was at seven. The guests were served tea and coffee and meat, both cold and boiled."

"And did Washington eat the same breakfast?"
The guard looked confused. "I don't know," he said. "I've only been here eight months."

This wasn't enough for George. Yet it seemed to him that the answer must be in the room itself. Maybe if he closed his eyes, the answer would come.

So George closed his eyes. He waited, and he listened. After a while he thought he heard a little crackling noise at the far end of the room. He guessed it might be the fire coming back in the fireplace. Then outside he heard a dog bark. Pompey, he thought. Or maybe Drunkard.

George squeezed his eyes even tighter and he listened even harder. Then he felt a shadow at the door. There was a very thin, ghosty-sounding whisper; George had to strain to hear it.

"I served the guests," the voice said. "Now you got the general's breakfast ready?"

George was so excited he snapped his eyes open. But there was no fire in the fireplace. There was no one talking; there were no signs of breakfast. He supposed he'd opened his eyes too soon, but when he tried to go back, it was no use. It was all gone. And the guard was giving him a funny look.

On Sunday afternoon George and his father and mother went home. They found George's grandmother and Miss Willing waiting together on the front porch.

"No luck," George reported. He was sorry that everyone was so disappointed, but he thought they should be planning what to do next.

Instead, Mr. Allen put his hand on George's shoulder. "It was a good try, son," he said. "You can't win them all."

"Sometimes there's nothing to do but give up," Mrs. Allen said.

George's grandmother said she guessed in the long run it didn't matter so much what George Washington ate.

George Allen looked at his family in amazement. *"Give up!"* he shouted. "You expect me to give up! George Washington's soldiers were starving, and they didn't give up. They were freezing, and they didn't give up. *What do you think I am?"*

George was so mad he slammed the screen door and went up to his room. But even upstairs he could hear them talking to Miss Willing about him. George stamped up to the attic. He sat down on the top step. It was quiet here. And very neat. He could see his grandmother had been working.

Next to him was a box filled with things he guessed his grandmother meant to throw away. On top of the box was an old stuffed dog. He remembered that dog. His name was Ginger. One ear was torn now, and the tail was hanging by a thread. Still, he was a good dog. George put him aside.

He looked back in the box. There was a bunch of old Batman comics. It was a good thing he'd come up here, he thought. No one should throw away old comics.

Under the comics George found a book. It was an old book, torn and beat-up-looking — probably his grandfather's, he thought, and it seemed a shame to throw it away. *The American Oracle*, the book was called, and it was written by the Honorable Samuel Stearns, whoever that was.

George whistled as he turned the pages. This honorable Samuel Stearns thought he knew *everything*. He told you how to choose a wife, how to kill bedbugs and how to keep from getting bald. He named the birds of North America (140), and he listed all the famous earthquakes since the year 17 (63 earthquakes). Then there was a chapter called "The Character of Washington."

George looked back at the title page where he knew he would find the date that the book was published.

"1791," he read. Samuel Stearns was living at the same time as Washington.

George turned back to the chapter on Washington. "Well, Mr. Stearns," George said, "if you know so much, kindly inform me about Washington's breakfast."

"Washington," Mr. Stearns wrote, "raised 7,000 bushels of wheat and 10,000 bushels of corn in one year."

"Okay, okay," George said. "That wasn't the question."

"Washington," Mr. Stearns continued, "is very regular, temperate, and industrious; rises winter and summer at dawn of day."

"Then what?" George asked.

"He breakfasts about seven," Mr. Stearns wrote, "on —"

Suddenly George let out a whoop. He put the book behind his back and clattered down the steps.

"Grandma!" he shouted. "When did you say you'd cook me George Washington's breakfast?"

"Boy, if you ever find out about that breakfast, I'll cook it right then no matter what time it is."

"Right this minute, for instance?"

"That's what I said."

George grinned. "Grandma," he said, "put on your apron." He brought the book out from behind his back.

"Washington," he read, "breakfasts about seven o'clock on three small Indian hoecakes and as many dishes of tea."

George passed the book around, and he thought he'd never seen people act as happy. All but his grandmother.

"George," she said, "I don't have the slightest idea what an Indian hoecake is."

George went to the dictionary. He looked under *H*. "Hoe-cake. A cake of cornmeal and water and salt baked before an open fire or in the ashes, originally on a hoe."

George's grandmother put on her apron. "I've cornmeal and water and salt," she said. "I guess I can make some Indian hoecakes."

George's father built a fire in the fireplace.

George's mother filled the kettle with water for the tea.

George said he'd go down to the basement for a hoe, but his grandmother stopped him. "You don't want me to cook these things on a *hoe*, do you?" she asked.

"That's what the dictionary says."

"The dictionary says *originally*. That means when hoecakes first came out. I expect they'd been around quite a while before Washington's time."

George wasn't sure. He wanted to do it right.

"Did you see a hoe in Washington's kitchen?"

George admitted there was no hoe there.

"All right then," his grandmother said. "Did you see any black iron griddles?"

George said that he had.

"That's what we'll use," his grandmother said. She mixed cornmeal and water in a bowl; she added salt; then she shaped the mixture in her hands to form little cakes.

Everyone sat around the fire to wait for breakfast. Pretty soon the tea kettle began to steam and the hoecakes began to turn a nice golden brown.

Then George's grandmother served George Washington's breakfast.

George took a bite of hoecake. It was pretty good, he thought. He looked at his mother and his father and his grandmother and Miss Willing all eating hoecakes together on a Sunday afternoon. George decided he felt more related to Washington than he'd ever felt in his whole life. It was as if George Washington were right there at the fireplace with them. And Drunkard at his feet.

There was only one trouble.

When George finished his three small hoecakes and his three cups of tea, he was still hungry. And if he was hungry, he thought, what about Washington? For a man who was six feet tall and the Father of His Country, it seemed like a skimpy breakfast.

"I hope Washington didn't have long to wait until lunch," he said. "I hope he had a nice big lunch to look forward to. A nice big one. I wonder what —"

But George never finished his sentence. His grandmother was standing up.

"George Washington Allen," she cried. "Don't you *dare*!" And she pointed her spatula at him.

"Not today," Miss Willing said. "The library is closed today."

"Okay." George grinned. "Not today."